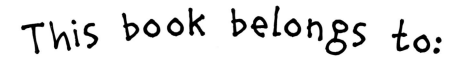

This book belongs to:

_ _

For Matthew.

OXFORD
UNIVERSITY PRESS

Great Clarendon Street, Oxford OX2 6DP

Oxford University Press is a department of the University of Oxford.
It furthers the University's objective of excellence in research, scholarship,
and education by publishing worldwide in

Oxford   New York

Auckland   Cape Town   Dar es Salaam   Hong Kong   Karachi
Kuala Lumpur   Madrid   Melbourne   Mexico City   Nairobi
New Delhi   Shanghai   Taipei   Toronto

With offices in

Argentina   Austria   Brazil   Chile   Czech Republic   France   Greece
Guatemala   Hungary   Italy   Japan   Poland   Portugal   Singapore
South Korea   Switzerland   Thailand   Turkey   Ukraine   Vietnam

Oxford is a registered trade mark of Oxford University Press
in the UK and in certain other countries

Just like Chri
you

CHARLOTTE MIDDLETON
presents

CHRISTOPHER'S Bicycle

a tale of cycling and recycling!

OXFORD
UNIVERSITY PRESS

Christopher Nibble loved
being in the garden.
It was usually so peaceful.

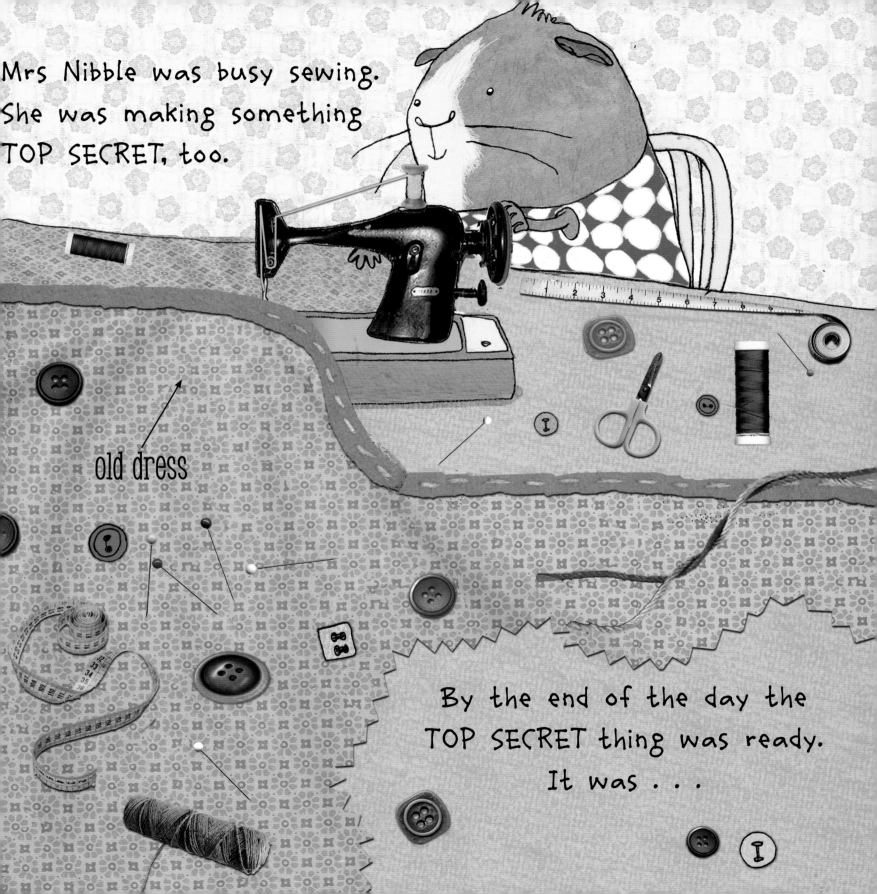

Mrs Nibble was busy sewing.
She was making something
TOP SECRET, too.

old dress

By the end of the day the
TOP SECRET thing was ready.
It was . . .

a bicycle for Christopher! He thought it was the best bicycle in the whole of Dandeville.

flowery panniers
(from Mrs
Nibble's dress)

honk!
honk!
horn

old picni
basket

go-faster
stripes

Mr Nibble's
shiny new
paintwork

'It's a recycled bicycle!' giggled his sister, Poppy.
And that gave Christopher an idea.

Early in the morning Christopher
pedalled off to Dandeville . . .

where he saw the lady from
the library. She was throwing
out yesterday's newspapers.

Christopher asked if he could take them. 'Please do!' said Miss Borrower.

After stopping at the bakery where
Mrs Choux was throwing out yesterday's
stale bread, Christopher asked Mr Rosetti
if he had any empty coffee jars.

He asked Posie from next door
and Poppy if they wanted to help.

While Christopher and Poppy found all sorts of things in the shed that they might need . . .

Posie searched online for recycling ideas.

They turned . . .

yesterday's newspapers into some very handy bags
(just the right size for taking your library book home).

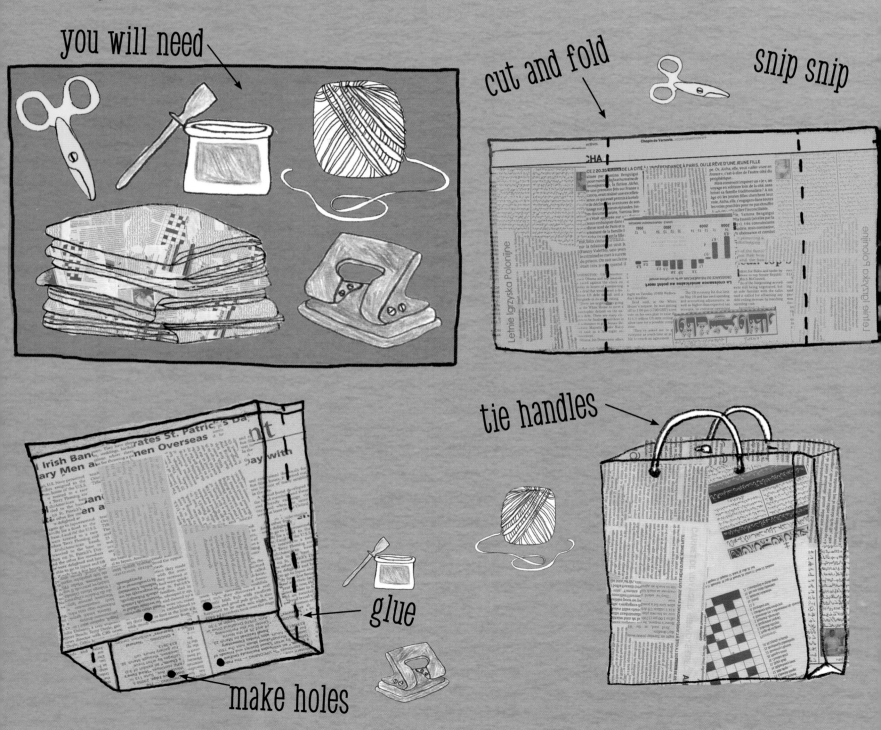

you will need

cut and fold

snip snip

tie handles

glue

make holes

They smeared the hard slices of
stale bread with suet and bird seed
to make hanging feeders.

And they turned empty coffee jars into bright vases, full of dandelions.

Then they loaded
Christopher's bicycle with
recycled goodies and set
off for Dandeville.

Miss Borrower was delighted
with her recycled book-bags.

'Wonderful!'
she said.

Mr Rosetti loved his dandelion vases.

'Bellissimo!'
he said.

And Madame Choux thought
the bird feeders were great.

'Marvellous!'
she said.

tweet!

tweet!

tweet!

Christopher, Posie, and Poppy
made everyone so excited
about recycling . . .

that they all decided to have a go.

And they held the Dandeville
Recycling Race to celebrate!